Ocho Rios

by Jesse Bier

Cover design by Debby Florence

Edited by Mackenzie Cole, BJ Soloy & Myrrah Dubey

editor@milltownepress.com

This is a work of fiction. Names, characters,

and incidents are the product of the author's

imagination. Any resemblance to actual events

or persons, living or dead, is entirely coincidental.

milltownepress.com

CHAPTER ONE

"What are we turning off here for?"

"Just like that," he said.

"My eye."

"No. My ear actually. Remember, I got this water in my ear? And I can't get rid of it."

He was off the coast highway now, going down a lone dirt road into Jamaica's back country.

"So," she asked, "where are we going all of a sudden? What's the connection?"

"You'll see." He clapped his left hand to his ear. "It's killing me."

"You're exaggerating. It's just a little water in your ear. You're a hypochondriac."

"Don't get fancy," he said. "If you think I'm crazy, just say so."

"You're crazy."

He put his hand back down to the wheel. "Then why are you with me?"

"I'm crazy, too."

He had reduced speed but was still going fast enough.

"It's killing me," he said again, his hand going halfway back up to his head but then down again. "It's murder." He laughed huskily, gripping the wheel. "As if *this* is going to do it."

"Stop it. Stop that."

"OK."

He drove for another mile or so on the ribbed road, finally coming to a little ramshackled cabin in a grove of peppermint trees, with four or five tethered goats roundabout in the clearing. He stopped.

"Sal," she said. "You *know* places like this spook me."

"It's all right. It's legit–or it's a legit con." He peered all about. "You didn't see his little sign on the main road? It said, 'Herbalist and Fortune Teller' with a hairpin arrow on it. I'll try *anything* now. Nothing that doctor gave me works, on top of their so-called pharmacists. I got this real pain, Maureen, in my eerie

2

canals. Like a toothache, you know what I mean? Maybe this old man in the bush knows something."

"Auntie Viola around the block in Paterson could lay her hands on your head just as easy. And cast the tea leaves, if you wanted extra hocus-pocus."

"That neighborhood phony," he said. "Anyway, we're not in Paterson, not nearly. C'mon." She didn't know if he meant, Get out of the car with him, or Don't go on talking anymore. He got out of the car, then she did, too. "And don't interfere. Let me just talk to the old gent."

"What'll you do," she found herself whispering, "if he's not old and he's just like Auntie Vi?"

"I'll turn back around and get out of here. All right? Now shut up, please."

"I hate when you say, 'Shut up.'"

"I said 'please.'"

"I hope you're just jumpy, about you-know-what, and that you're not changing character on me."

"Now who's exaggerating? Just shush."

He was at the front screen door and knocked.

A slight, cocoa-colored, sweet-faced girl of twelve or so opened the door and her big eyes. "Yes?"

"Can we see the herb man?" Maureen poked him. "Please."

"Come in," the girl said, slowly opening the door.

And they went in.

CHAPTER TWO

It was just as Sal envisioned—not a large plenipotentiary Auntie Viola but a little old wizened black man, sitting in a small rocker in a corner of the room that came after the porch and kitchen. He was rocking gently, almost imperceptibly, near a small window. He looked up.

"My name is Bianco," Sal said, "I was wondering if you could help me. My ear hurts, and it's ruining my time here on your beautiful island."

The old man commenced nodding and indicated two cane-backed chairs for the couple, who sat. His voice was very quiet and low.

"What?"

"It's this left ear, with water in it from swimming in the ocean. It pains me. Very much."

The old man stopped nodding. He looked at them both gravely. Then, in a hoarse, low whisper he asked Sal, "How long, mahn?"

"Ten, eleven days. Swimmers Ear didn't help. I saw a medical doctor five days ago, he didn't help either. Seems it's hurting *more* now. Can't sleep."

"Emmalina," the old man called for the girl, who came. "Bring my small satch', and water." While they waited, he said nothing. He looked at Sal. Then he said, "Bianco. Ital or Spanid?"

"Italian American."

"Spanids here in Jamaica, ol' days. Fight with Englis. No Itals."

"No," Sal said. "No Americans then, either."

"Americans now," the old man said, gravely.

But then the girl brought him his satchel, from which he took a box, more like a little chest, which he set on its back, with two latched front portals that he opened as he kept it, flat, on his lap. He peered inside it, at cubby holes in it. The girl came back with a glass of water, which she placed carefully on a low table beside him, and left. Sal thought he would have to swallow a potion. He worried about the cleanliness of the glass.

The old man fingered several packets and presently lifted one from the chest. He held it aloft a moment, nodded, then folded the end of it tightly over whatever powder was inside. He handed it to his guest. Then he closed the chest, slowly latching the little doors.

Sal took the packet. He and Maureen sat there.

The old man reached for the glass of water. Sal leaned forward. But the old man simply took a drink for himself and put the glass back down on the low table. For a moment a light may have come into his eyes.

Sal said, "Oh," sitting back.

No one said anything.

Maureen stood up slowly, then Sal.

"How should he take it?" she asked, pointing to the packet Sal still held.

"When you go back to hotel," the old man said, "make a paste. He should put it in his ear with his finger. No sticks, just little finger. Then tomorrow, one time."

"That's all?" Sal asked. "That's it?"

When the old man nodded, they nodded with him.

"How much do I owe you?" Sal asked.

The old man shrugged.

"No," Sal said, "tell me."

The old man shook his head ever so slightly. "You say, you give."

Sal took out his wallet. "Oh, I forgot," he said to Maureen, "I've got four dollars is all, besides the travelers checks. You've got the heavy cash."

In the inside pocket of her purse, along with the wad of hundreds, she found loose fifties, a few twenties, and some fives and tens. "What'll it be, Sal?"

"Give him a twenty for now."

"For now?"

"Maybe I'll be back, if it works."

"For what?"

Sal laughed. "Maybe to pension him off, with a fifty."

They paid him and said good-bye. The old man smiled weakly, maybe thanked them in his mumbling. His eyes glittered. They left him in his chair with the herb box on his lap, sunshine coming through the small window on his sparse grizzled head.

Sal gave Emmalina one of his singles, and they got back in the rental car. He waved to her, backed up, then turned around and pulled out. He drove to the coast highway and straight to their rented villa just west of Ocho Rios.

CHAPTER THREE

Two days later the ear ache was gone. Completely gone.

Sal walked around the king-size bed in the big bedroom, pranced even, then jumped on the bed once and back down. "I feel OK."

"Great," Maureen said, "but you're a little hyperactive."

"You know why," he said. "Anyway, the ear's fine. You know what I'm going to do?"

"Go in for a dip."

"Yeah, but after that."

"Go back to the herb man in the woods."

"How did you know?"

"I would've guessed. But you said so."

"When? Do I talk in my sleep now?"

"You said maybe you'd pension him off, remember? That malarkey. You meant, if the potion worked, you might try the fortune-telling, too."

"Oh. That's right."

"And you laugh at bozos and floozies going to Aunt Viola."

"This is different."

"Of course."

"None of your heavy metal."

"What?" After a pause Maureen threw a pillow at him. "Godalmighty! Irony, you mean iron-y! And the thing is, I can't tell when you're really joking or not."

"I can't either," he said. "I don't know all I'm saying sometimes."

"Yes," Maureen said, "and it isn't always funny. Like 'your beautiful island.' You said that when you first met that old man."

"It's true, isn't it?"

"It was the kind of thing you never say, I mean to make an impression on somebody. It's not like you, Sal."

"Maybe I'm improving–changing for the better."

"Not like that, and so Waspy."

Sal had subsided, was almost pensive. "You're right," he said. "I gotta get a hold on myself. I'm still going back there, though."

"I hate the idea."

"You don't have to go. But I've got to. Hey, you see how the cure worked? Total. And fast. I don't know how he does it, but it stands to reason he's worth the other visit."

"It's spooky."

"Because it's so poor and dilapidated? C'mon."

"That's part of it. All of a sudden we drive out of here—"her wave took in the room, the deluxe house, the ocean view—"and pow into somebody else's deep-down grind of a life. If you want to know, I'm embarrassed. And the other part is, yes, scared."

"Don't go."

"I don't want you out of my sight any more than necessary. On your business maybe in Montego or Ocho, but not in those woods. It's also like a moonshine place back there."

"You never saw a moonshine operation."

"I can imagine."

"Now *you're* going off, Maureen."

"Oh? Maybe the herbs are illegal."

Sal laughed out loud. He often had a strong, boisterous laugh. It was not displeasing to her.

"Listen, College Girl," he said suddenly, in earnest, "how come it's 'erbs, what about the *h*? I know you're not putting me on. But why is that?"

"Search me," she said.

"All right," he said, approaching and putting his hands all over.

*   *   *

Afterward she said, "Do me a favor."

"No," he said. "I'm out of here! This afternoon."

"Don't, Sal. Maybe the f-, the fortune is illegal too." She had almost said future.

"I said you were going off. Bye-bye, I'm going for a swim now."

"Don't forget ear plugs."

"Oh, for the dip."

"That too," she said.

"You meant, for the fortune-telling?" He slid back the double-doors to the patio and the beach beyond, going out. "You're losing it, Maureen."

"That was a long time ago," she started calling out after him, but it came out a whisper.

CHAPTER FOUR

When Sal drove back to the woods, Maureen was in tow. That was just as well, it turned out.

"The ear's all better," he told the old man. "I came back– excuse me, please, what's your name?"

"Clive."

"I came back, Mr. Clive–"

"My firs' name, mahn."

"Oh. Sure. My name's Salvatore. This is Maureen." The nodding took place. "The reason I–"

"You want your fortune now?"

"That's it. Will you do that for me, too? I'll pay you enough."

Clive raised a withered hand. He kept looking steadily at Salvatore Bianco. Then he folded down the two end fingers and thumb of the raised hand. For a moment both Sal and Maureen thought he was making a V for victory.

"Two," the old man said. "Two fortunes."

Sal glanced at Maureen. "Here comes the con?" To Clive he said, "I just want one fortune."

"Same price," the old man said. "No con. Two for one."

"Yeah? Let's decide the price first. How much?"

The old man shrugged, as he had on the first visit.

Sal turned to Maureen, speaking low to her. "He's got modest prices for locals, of course, unless it's an emergency. But, again, he's smart enough to leave it to the white fella because I probably overpaid for the prescription. He's counting on that again, and that's all right, my ear's perfectly OK, and this may be worth it, too; another, you-might-say, emergency."

He turned back to Clive. "All right. Leave it to me."

They were in the same room as before, seated the same way. It was the same sun streaming through the same little window. Today it made a sort of cloudy halo on the old man's white frizzled head. All the while the old man had been looking unwaveringly at Sal–peering, studying. Now he gravely shook his head.

"You go," he said to Sal. He pointed outside the room they were in. "I tell your woman firs'."

"What??"

"The firs' one, I tell it to her. She tells you later. Then–"

"What?!"

"–we'll see if I'm right."

"On this first one, he means," Maureen interpreted. "He's testing you, and you'll be testing him. Then, maybe, you'll come back for the second."

"I'm not budging–"

14

"Sal, either let's get in the car and get out of here, or you go in the hall, or kitchen, and wait. It'll probably be a minute."

So, Sal thought, Maureen was still sitting and not, in fact, on her feet, heading to the car with him, seizing the opportunity? It had taken; she was fixed there, too.

Sal sauntered into the hall, closing the door behind him.

CHAPTER FIVE

In the car Sal said, "He told *you* my fortune?" They were jouncing up the ribbed dirt road to the coastal highway. "Why the hell is that?"

"It's *his* way."

"It's *my* fortune. What was it anyway?"

"I can't tell you until we get back. He said so."

"Why? Why the hell why?"

"I don't know. Maybe it's because he thought you might crash the car."

CHAPTER SIX

"OK," he said in the villa. "What?"

"He's telling you two futures."

"Yeah, same price and all. I remember."

"This is your near-future."

"OK, OK. *What* is it?"

"That you'll go back to see him."

Sal slapped his thigh, hard. "Bianco, little ol' Jeeves down here has taken you."

"Jeeves?"

"His name."

"His name's Clive."

"Whatever it is, now I'm *not* going back." Sal sucked in some air. "I didn't pay for this yet. Good for me."

"Oh?"

"I was only going to pay, two-for-one, on the far-future."

"Very smart."

"If I've got one."

"Sal."

"Sorry. I meant if *we've* got one."

"Don't."

"I'm more jumpy about you than me. I don't care about me. But they'll get you, too–with me, or after. That's what I worry about."

"Stop. I feel the same, the exact same feeling. So I know. But we've got to stop it. We did what we did, and let's try to get away with it, just as we planned. All right?"

"All right."

"And let's forget the little old man in the woods. No more side trips."

"No. But give him credit, the backcountry con artist. Giving me jive like this."

"That's it!" Maureen said, lighting up her terrific smile.

"What?"

"Jive. You said jive." She came over to poke and tickle him.

"Yes...?"

"That's how you mixed up the name: Clive - Jive - Jeeves. That's how your mind can work."

"Oh."

"It's deeper than 'oh.' Look at your attitude, underneath. You're suspicious of him–"

"Sure."

"And you think of him–back there in his country cabin, and all–as less than you. Also he's on hire to you."

"You mean–that I think–way down–he's my valet. G'wan."

"Don't tell me to g'wan, I hate it."

"Then stay. And tell me something else, big psychologist–"

"I'm not big."

"You've got 'em."

"You're gross sometimes. In a middle of a conversation, is that what gets into your head?"

"I hope so. Hey, listen, the Big Bazooms against the Big D– that's only natural. I'm still alive, *still* living."

"Good. That's what I like to hear. Keep that thought."

"Tell me something else, about the old guy in the bush. How come he could supposedly tell even half my fortune if he didn't read tea leaves or something? What's the basis?"

"Oh, he read something."

"What?"

"Your face. He was reading your face, Sal, the whole time."

"That's the basis?"

"It's better than Auntie Viola, for my money."

"My money, too," Sal said. "*Our* money. Two million smackeroos. All we have to do is work the transfer and live out this month."

"Sal–"

"Sorry," Sal raised both hands, warding off reproach. "I just meant *that's* the future I wanted to know. But not from any old man of the woods reading my crow's feet or zeroing in on my dimples–"

"And your cleft chin. God, you *are* the best looking man I know, that much is true."

"I'm not going back to a palm reader that's graduated to noggins. Flattery ain't necessary. Don't worry, I'm staying right here."

"Good-bye, Jives," she said, waving her hand to mid-island.

"And hello you," Sal said, advancing upon her in no uncertain terms.

"I was wondering when you were going to get back to that," she said, her waving still up, then draped around his neck.

CHAPTER SEVEN

Instead of dozing as usual, Sal walked around the room, looked at their inlet, studied it, walked about some more.

"Sal," Maureen said, "relax."

"I'm OK."

"I know, but relax." He still paced. "You said there's nothing you can do right now. You're waiting for the second laundering."

"As long as it isn't a wash-out." He looked in her direction. "I'm a little nervous. This isn't exactly the Witness Protection Program. It's a Fugitive Protection Plan of our own. And we don't have any government behind us. Still, we've got it mostly figured. What am I talking so much? It's going through, it's all right."

"Remember what you always say: if it's a done deal or in the works–"

"–don't look back. The difference between a man and a woman–I mean, a man and a boy–is he never looks back, doesn't second-guess himself, never worries it. Your 'uncle' taught me that, he did."

She did not say anything.

"Maybe we picked the wrong island to wait it out and get the 'change.'"

"Sal."

"Right, never second-guess. I just said. It's only that things keep happening or get into my mind by themselves. Hey, as soon as we got here: the Holiday Inn at Montego Bay–who would've thought?"

Who would have thought of armed guards? At a seaside family Caribbean resort? Nobody bothered to tell them, at the reception desk or anywhere else. So Sal and Maureen went down a corridor, made a turn, and there stood a man cradling an Uzi machine gun. A thought flashed through Sal's helpless and hapless mind: They found us already! He could not believe it; but there the man was–*some*body, with a cannon, on the look-out. For what? Maybe for Salvatore Bianco, for only Salvatore Bianco. It was impossible for Sal to deny his reflex, to make a move toward the man before the man could bring the Uzi level, but then he checked himself, kept his cool, before the man noticed anything.

Now Sal said, "Maybe I'm still a little tense from that."

"I was startled, too," Maureen said. "But now we know: hotels and places have got guards posted. We've got the picture."

"You take Kingston," Sal went on, "I'm prepared for anything over there. But not on this tourist coast, I thought. They can't have crime *here*."

"That's what the armed guards are for."

"Big help. Twenty miles from here, four guys carry subs, break in on a villa, a private party going on, and rob a dozen guests, everything but their brassieres and jockey shorts."

"It couldn't happen in Montclair?"

"C'mon, Maureen, this is a lot worse. And those two Canadian girls we read about, raped in their condo over by Priory. Armed guys again. More armed guys than armed guards."

"Sal, you *know* somebody got raped in their house in Tenafly. You're losing your perspective; you're losing your grip."

"Oh no, I got a grip," Sal said. "Including my own piece."

For a split second Maureen thought he had turned obscene, again, and witless. But he brought out a .38 pistol from a pocket of the terry cloth lounge jacket he had on.

"Where did you–?"

"Back in Montego. It's a Russian rip-off of a German police piece. You know, when I saw all the Ladas they drive on this island, I figured the place must be loaded with other stuff from Cold War days. The island's flooded with Soviet surplus. So I got around last Tuesday, when you were getting your hair done, and found what I was looking for, not far from the airport, matter of fact. The cabbies knew. Cheap enough, too."

"Don't shoot a guard."

"Funny gal," he said. "But, you know, that's just what a hit man could be. *That's* why I tensed at the Holiday Inn."

"Well, you'll be all right," she said, wanting to mollify him and wanting to believe it.

"Good," Sal said. "I need a friend in a foreign country."

"I'm your friend," she said.

And they went out for a tan together on their enclosed, snug little beach.

CHAPTER EIGHT

They lolled around the next day, too. Maureen made an omelet with jalapeno peppers, as Sal liked, for lunch.

"Not a bad life," he said.

It's paradise," she said. "How· much longer do we have here?"

"A few weeks. We can't *stay* here. Eventually He'll have people, even PIs, checking on every which island in the Caribbean. We got 100 K on us; the rest is going through Cayman."

"Doesn't He know Cayman?"

"Now who's the worrywart?" Sal said. "But *we're* not there, are we? Only the rest of the money's there, working through to Switzerland. Then we'll go, too."

"But Switzerland? Hasn't He got to be on to Switzerland, too, eventually?"

"No. I told you before, it's not regular Switzerland. Listen, if you're thinking of Ireland again, forget it. He'll have a special look-out there, because of you–and on Sicily, because of me. Forget about Rio, it's too usual. And your idea of New Zealand because it's so far away–we'd stick out too much and, anyway, no place is too far. No, we just have to out-think Him. We're heading for the Ticino."

"Italian-speaking Switzerland. I don't know…you get Him thinking hard, and long enough, and with experts to talk to all the time, and you can't be sure what He won't come up with."

"Nobody'll come up with the outskirts of Lugano. And He's not forever, remember. The next one will try, too, but less hard, less often. Finally, we'll be written off. Meanwhile, we get new names and passports here. Then, when the money's in Lugano, we go. We settle into the whole of Ticino. I speak Italian. You've got some vocabulary, and–"

"Not that I can use for shopping."

"You'll pick up what lingo you need. We'll be OK. For a while you have to dye your hair. I'm starting a beard. We'll pass. Over there we'll take trips to Milano–"

"There's a track there?"

"And European football, if you want to know. But never mind the betting, the Scala is there, I want to see it, and we'll go to Vienna for coffee and cakes, and go to Zurich and Geneva. We'll have the Alps. Beaches down in Viareggio. We'll be in good shape. As long as we hang out in the one spot He doesn't penetrate. All we have to do is–"

"What exactly?"

"Live until then."

CHAPTER NINE

In the afternoon, on their little cozy beach, Sal kept eyeing the high bluff on the east side. He was scuffing sand, looking up.

"They'd use a Tommy or a shotgun. Spray effect. No high-powered, pinpoint stuff. That's for the other guys, the SWATs. Too far for a shotgun, so they'd use a Tommy."

"You're doing it again, Sal. If it isn't one of us, it's the other. Let's just stop it."

"It's the not knowing."

"Welcome to life. When has it been different?"

"You'll always stand by me?"

"Is it OK if I sit?"

"Maureen, sometimes you kid at the wrong time."

"You," she said, "come over here. Stop looking up there–at nothing–and stretch out here next to me." He did so. "I'll stand by you, I'll sit by you, I'll lay by you. OK?"

"*By?*"

"Now, now."

"We have a good time in bed, I'll say that. And out of bed, for that matter. You remember the hallway once, in Passaic? And the basement pool table?"

"I remember. You remember the sex and positions. I remember the passion."

"What's the difference?"

"God, I wish you hadn't said that."

"Why?"

"It creates distance."

"Oh. Because this is a kind of honeymoon and, like some other couples–because it must happen sometimes–we've found, all alone together, that we made a mistake?"

"I didn't say that. I don't mean that. There are just man-woman differences, I suppose. Even between close people. We're close, aren't we?"

"Sure. And we'll actually get married, over there. Hey, the whole first year will be our honeymoon. OK? But..."

"Yes?"

"The passion part. You got to remember, Babe, it was secret, forbidden, dangerous. That's where the passion came in, at least extra. I don't figure you can have that all the time, when it's out in the open. Even here, though we're under pressure, it's not the same."

She patted his head.

"You're right. Actually you're smart sometimes. What'll we have then?"

"Just sex and love."

"In that order?"

Sal leaned up on his elbows. "No. Now it's become the other way around."

It was just the right thing to say, plus he meant it.

"I'll take it," she said.

He stood up. "You know what? I'm Jack, like in Jack and the Beanstalk. I steal the Giant crazy, *and* I get the Princess, only I don't chop anything down, I just try to get the hell gone. *With* the golden harp."

"I thought you were going to say golden girl."

"*And* the Goldwyn girl, sure. But, like I said, Maureen, you have to go brunette, soon."

"All right," she said after a quick laugh. "You going to change your name to Jack?"

"Symbolizing the money? No. I've already picked out both names. Mine will still be Italian, in keeping."

"And I'll be in keeping, too?"

"Funny girl," he said. "I *said* I'd marry you."

He looked down at her. She thought, Oh God, he's handsome, just standing there, the blue lagoon behind him. And so well-built, not *too* bulging from the gym machines. Behind him, the sea; beyond that,the lagoon opened wide, farther out, glinting bright.

"I'm going to swim," he said.

He put in his earplugs and then waded into the water slowly, patting water all over himself. Then, all at once, he dived in and came up unexpectedly far off. He was a good, strong swimmer.

When he got back, she tossed a towel up to him. He dried off, then draped the towel over his head and neck.

"I could be Abou-ben-Bianco," he said, glancing up at the bluff again. "Especially with a beard. Our neighbor, on that side, is some sheik, I found out. Only he's hardly ever home. Nobody there now."

"What's on the other side? Can you see when you swim out as far as you do?"

"Yeah, there's something visible, about a quarter mile away. There's a big pontoon boat and little rubber rafts at a sort of landing. I found out about that too, it's what they call an Elderhassle."

"Elder-hostel!"

"Hostile?"

She held her head in her hands for a moment. Then, looking up at him, she said, "I already told you that you're not dumb. In fact, you're smart. But, Sal, you're ignorant. What I want to know is, confidentially, between lovers and friends, how come, smart as you are, you're so ignorant?"

"I never paid attention in school. I just didn't care. So I never learned much."

"They never kept you back?"

"No. I got suspended a few times. Never kept back and never expelled."

"How come?"

"You see, I would teach other kids how to play cards. In the schoolyard."

"And bet?"

"Yep. You see, the reason they never threw me out is that I did too good at arithmetic."

"But not English."

"You know what I think," Sal went right on, "I think I was actually performing a service for them, out in the yard, teaching the kids how to count."

"For which they forgave the gambling?"

"Oh, it was just pennies. Hey, nowadays, kids who are the age I was then are dealing drugs; they carry rods into the school. Me, I had a deck of small playing cards. I was harmless."

"I know. You still are, basically. The main thing wrong with you is that you just didn't get an education."

"Not much. A mistake. Hey, that doesn't mean I don't ever think. On my own. Ask me. About anything."

"All right," Maureen said, "but not now. I just want to lie here and look at you and at the water."

"That's the thing to do," he said.

She looked at their snug cove again and the scintillant sea out where the breakers were.

She could also smell jasmine, a big wafting hint of it on the soft air.

"We've got this," she said.

"Yes."

Without her noticing, he shot another glance at the neighboring bluff. Then he dried himself completely and lay down next to her again. He put the towel over his eyes.

CHAPTER TEN

After breakfast the next morning, he said, "I'm going back."

"Over my dead body."

"You're something."

"It was a slip," she said.

"You make them all the time. God, we're getting to be alike! It's going to turn out incestuous."

"What are you talking about?"

"Nothing. I don't want you to come."

"You don't even say where."

"It could be Ocho Rios. Maybe business in Montego."

"I know where. I know where. I didn't know when. I *hoped* it wouldn't be just now."

"I don't follow."

"Never mind, I'm being what they call cryptic. Cancel that," she said, knowing he'd hear crypt, "I just don't want you to go back. I thought you finally decided that Clive was a con."

"I got second or third thoughts. Listen, Maureen, whatever way it works out in the end, I never meant that the old man–con, or not–was less than me. Nobody's more but nobody's less than me. Anyhow, I'm going. You don't have to."

"No, I'll go. I'm–" she looked out the living room window and muttered to herself– "between the devil and the deep blue sea."

CHAPTER ELEVEN

When they broke off the shore highway to the herbalist, Maureen said, "Stop the car. I've got to tell you something."

He slowed down, then pulled the car up against a road wall of heavy hibiscus, and stopped.

"You spooked again?"

"Not by the place. It's the old man's prediction."

"That I'd come back?"

"That you'd come back *today*."

"Today?"

"Exactly today. He said, 'The mahn come in tree days.' And here it is, on the button."

"So? It's just a coincidence."

"If that isn't scary, what is?"

"You must be out of my mind," he said, his tone absolutely level. He chuffed rather than laughed. "Cool down. So he made a prediction, so what?"

"I wasn't supposed to tell you this detail." Maureen sighed way down, deeply. "He's reading you, Sal. It's uncanny. An exact fix."

"Maureen, Maureen. If he'd said yesterday, or tomorrow, he'd have an excuse handy. Part of the c-game. So he happened to hit it right, that's all. He's not the Pope." He re-started the car.

"Then why the hell are you going at all?"

"Good question." He resumed the country road, down toward the cabin.

"Let's turn around," she urged. Sal kept going. "Let's go back." He didn't. "If he's right, it's scary. If he's wrong, it's a waste of time." Sal kept on, lurching here and there over ruts and around eruptive stones. "Why?"

"My ear," Sal said. "He cured me."

"Yes," she said. "There's that."

CHAPTER TWELVE

At the cabin, they found the old man sitting on a rocker on the porch, as if waiting for them, rocking gently in the dappled sun.

When they got out of the car, Sal called out, "I'm back, Clive."

Clive wound himself slowly and unsteadily out of the rocker. He waved a hand feebly and then called to inside the cabin, and Emmalina and another older woman came out to help him in. All three smiled shyly. After the old man was installed again in his room, in his place by the window, Sal and Maureen sat across from him once more.

"Far fortune?" the old man asked.

"Yes," Sal said.

"Only one question allowed. What you want to know?"

"Am I going to die?"

The old man nodded once, decisively. He was not smiling. His mouth had tightened and was slightly puckered.

Sal did not say anything. He was looking back steadily at the old man. Nobody said anything.

Maureen said, under her breath to Sal, "That's a crock. Ask *when*."

"Sooner or later?" Sal asked Clive. "Part of the same question."

"Sooner than later."

"How soon?"

"It's up to you."

"What?" Sal smiled. "Old mahn, you're taking me."

Clive shook his head once but kept looking in Sal's direction, his eyes now veiled, almost closed. His whole face was tight. Both Sal and Maureen leaned forward. Slowly the old man extended his hand. Sal sat back.

"Pay him, Sal. It's not for shaking hands. It's fee time."

"Here's fifty," Sal said to the old man. "Make it sweet, and there's another."

Clive's hand folded over the bill and withdrew. Sal laughed outright.

Maureen said, "You can't bribe him." Deep inside the words there was a terror that nobody could hear, not Sal, not even Maureen herself, the tone or tremor slipping away so fast, especially under Sal's renewed laugh, that she did not know she had felt what she felt.

"Is that so?" Sal asked Clive, standing up.

The old man started nodding. "Time is over," he said.

Sal stared at him.

"Not you, Sal," Maureen said. "*His* time–the séance is over." Then she stood up, too.

They said good-bye and drifted out of the room and out of the house and off the porch back to the car. Sal was the slowest he'd been in driving the country road back to the coast highway. They did not exchange a syllable.

Then she said, "Why did you say 'mahn' that once to him?"

"I just did. I don't know why I say things sometimes. What's the difference?"

Maureen subsided or collapsed into the back of her seat. "I don't know. Maybe it made a difference to him."

After a minute he said, "What?"

"You're making these mistakes."

"It was just talk. You know me."

She had the standard reply ready but did not use it. He may have been grateful for that if he was still paying attention.

CHAPTER THIRTEEN

It was turning out to be a long month.

"This is jail," Maureen complained, "a good-looking jail, but jail, if we don't get out more. I mean not just driving around and going to fortune tellers."

He agreed that, by now, he had enough of a beard, and she'd become a transitional redhead, and they could go out and eat and do some things. They had dinner at a fancy place in Priory. She had jerked goat but he took the pork.

"High class place," Sal said during the meal. "Good-looking people in here." He turned directly to her. "But you're the best-looking woman."

Maureen started to say something.

"Don't thank me, "he said. "Statement of fact."

"Maybe I'll stay a redhead."

"Two weeks of Rita Hayworth," he said, "then on the plane and outta here."

"Whatever you say. Rita Hayworth? You're getting *back* your sense of humor."

"C'mon. You look really good. You know it. What was that, getting *back* my sense of humor?"

"I was thinking of that false fire alarm we had the other night."

"Oh, that."

They had scurried out of the house. She had put her nightie back on and run out like that, but he was still naked. Except for the .38 in his hand. It flashed through Sal's mind that He had set fire to the house to smoke them out, and so he had grabbed his gun. And there they were. No fire. Just a faulty battery in the alarm. Maureen started laughing, uncontrollably, with Sal standing buck naked, ready to shoot the moon.

"But you didn't see anything funny," she said. "I'm glad you're getting back to normal <u>now</u>."

"Don't worry."

At the end of the meal, Sal took out a cigar and lit up, very ceremoniously.

"Sal Bianco, you don't smoke."

"This isn't real smoking. Also, it's another dodge. And maybe it's my sense of humor coming back."

"Only if it blows up." She could have bitten her tongue, the whole tongue.

All he acknowledged was: "It's a Cuban cigar. They got plenty of them here, of course, smuggled in. This could cost twenty-five dollars in the States." He puffed grandly.

"Where did you get it? When?"

"A place in Montego Bay. When you were getting your hair done again. I do things then."

"You certainly do. Transacting business, or buying a pistol, or locating Havana cigars." She sighed. "You certainly find your way around. I can't do that."

"Yes, you could. If you had to. With me around, you just leave it to me."

"I do," she said, "I do."

Sal brushed aside the cigar smoke and looked into her eyes. "Wait until Lugano," he said, "and I'll get you the engagement *and* wedding rings."

CHAPTER FOURTEEN

The next day Sal took Maureen about a mile west of the Elderhostel compound to St. Ann's Polo Club, where Jamaica East was playing Narragansett. They looked at the horses, bought some ices, then sat in the small unpretentious stands on one side of the field and watched the game.

"It's soccer with sticks," Sal said, "on an even bigger field, naturally. You like the Yank snobs or the natives?"

"Natives? They're as white as us. The only blacks are the handlers we saw."

"Which side do you like?"

"Can't we just watch the game?"

"I never just watch a game. You like the green jerseys or the red?"

"There's-look-a girl playing on the green side."

"Yep. The times they are changing. I'll be back in a minute."

He was longer than that. It was a lovely day. Maureen saw one goal, then a second scored.

When Sal came back, she said, "Did you place a bet?"

"This is not the races," Sal said. "I had to find side action."

"Did you bet on green?"

"I did. Just for fun." He grinned. "If there's one place He'd have them looking for me, it would be at a track. *Never* at a polo field." He laughed in his good strong voice– gleefully, really happy.

He bought her another ice, Jamaica East lost (but Sal won on a point-spread), and they got down from the stands and he went someplace and collected. When he came back, they stood for awhile looking at the horses coming back in. The horses were beautiful: not a sway back among them, all of them sleek and straight, sweating as they filed in. They were sweating now– glittering, big, powerful mounts. When one halted near her, Maureen carefully stroked his head, and he snuffled amiably. It was really a lovely day.

And she had felt exceptionally good before, up until Sal had mentioned the track. Couldn't they have one day without a reference, one whole day? Otherwise, it had been their best day: unthreatening, soft, delightful.

CHAPTER FIFTEEN

Another day they decided to go to the river float. On the way it was her turn to point out a sign, a big highway poster directed to the Jamaicans themselves: Be Good To Tourists.

"Does that make you feel OK?" Sal asked.

"I don't know. Right out in the open like that is good. But something's wrong."

Sal drummed the steering wheel. "Think!" he said. "Talk about hostile."

"What do you mean?"

"Why would they say Be Good if being good and pleasant–"

"–was natural? I get that. But maybe they're just reminding themselves."

"C'mon. Listen, remember when He had His lung out?"

"Yes."

"For weeks, after He came back from the hospital, what would He say?"

"He said, 'Breathe that air! Breathe it! Don't it feel good to breathe! Breathe the air!'"

"Right. Did He ever say that before?"

"No. But what's the connection?"

"The connection is, you don't talk so much about something natural, something, anything–"

"–that you take for granted."

"That's it. Like normal breathing. Or being good and friendly. You only brag or shout about what isn't natural anymore."

"You're on to something," she said, but she teased him: "so, they can't breathe here?"

"If I wasn't driving," he answered, "I'd sock you one." But he was grinning broadly.

"You wouldn't."

"No, I wouldn't. Well, maybe I'd punch your arm. You know when I fell in love with you?"

"The first time you punched my arm."

"Yes! And you me. He asked me to take you to the movies, and we saw Moonstruck, and we poked elbows into one another and punched arms. I liked you from the first time we locked eyes, but I loved you starting at the Cineplex."

"Sometimes you almost make me bawl."

"Don't," he said. "The windshield wipers only work on the outside."

CHAPTER SIXTEEN

This is what happened on Martha Brae River. Sal almost killed the light-tinctured pole man on the raft.

First of all, when they parked at the departure installation, there were no other cars or hotel vans around just then. Maureen felt a little uneasy (maybe Sal did too, looking over his shoulder a couple of times), but they got into a picturesque long raft anyhow and lazied down the mudbrown sluggish rivulet.

About half-way down, the poler tried to sell them a miniature toy raft for six dollars. He wouldn't take no for an answer. While Sal lay resting in the bow of the raft, Maureen on her bench at the stern declined the sale. But, the poler asked, didn't they have any children? "Not yet." Not little nieces or nephews? "Not that we're going to see soon." Not even for five dollars? "Not even for four." That was that until, in a very slow umbrageous passage, the poler unfolded a large sharp knife, while they just floated, and he began scraping out a gourd. Some of the shavings fell on Sal. "No gourd either," Maureen said. The poler put down the gourd and pointing, maybe brandishing the knife, said that he would let the toy raft go at three dollars. Maybe stretching somewhat, he could have reached down near his feet and slit Sal's throat. Instead, Sal reached up all at once and grabbed the poler's wrist.

As Sal rose, slowly but surely, he gripped the man's arm and twisted it so that the knife fell overboard. Then Sal let go and swiftly stood up all the way and turned on the poler, at the same time reaching for his neck. The man started to explain but found himself in a powerful vise, being choked and simultaneously lifted off his feet into the blue air. A macaw cried in the trees. The man heard that, perhaps the last sound he'd ever hear, and he saw bolts of blue before his vision hooded. His legs thrashed but, curiously, his arms went entirely limp, dangling, not sharing in the convulsion of the rest of him. A small man in Sal's sinewy grip, he started turning crimson on the way to purple. Maureen shouted, "Let him go, Sal! Now, now!" Relaxing his hold, while looking circumspectly all about, Sal brought the pole man back down to the platform of the raft and let go.

"Listen," Sal said, "don't look away! Listen." Now they were lazily floating out of the dense-treed passage. "Somebody hire you to do that?"

"No," the poler finally spat out. "By myself. I always try dat."

"OK," Sal said, still looking all around. With his elbow and inner lower arm he felt his travel packet at his hip where he kept the gun. "Now listen again: you stand up now and get that pole and push us down and shut up. Shut up, now and later."

"Yes," the poler had his cracked voice back, and some of his normal color too, but his throat and neck were vividly bruised. "Yes."

And that was scenically and eventfully that. They arrived at the take-out station, where a jitney brought them back up to their car in the parking lot, now half full.

Walking over to the car, Maureen said, "You were thirty seconds from Murder Two."

"He was just going to pass out, first."

"My God, Sal."

He stopped in his tracks and said, "Listen," to her too, which she did. The truth is, instant decisive full action on Sal's part, even naked on their beach the other night, the *atto puro* side of him, was a powerful attractant for her, almost as much as his good looks. He spoke low but intently to her, though nobody else was around them. "How could I know, for sure, if there wasn't more in it than the cheap trick he was pulling? Could I know for sure? Could I?"

"I guess not."

They resumed their way to the car.

"The poor pole man," she said.

"He's OK. Right now, he's glad he's alive. He'll knock off his con game for two, three days and then, feeling better, start all over again."

They got into the car.

"He was not very Good To Tourists," Maureen said.

"Nobody with dreadlocks is going to heed that or any other sign," Sal said; "he just didn't judge us right, especially me snoozing there."

"One thing for sure," Maureen said, "*he* didn't read your face."

Sal was grinning again. "No. And I got more beard now. Even Jeeves would have trouble." He started the car and drove out of there. "The poler will have to get another knife. It was a big one, did you notice?"

"I noticed."

"Small men wear big belt buckles and sport big knives. Hey, you woman: you ever notice belt buckles?"

Maureen did not say. She was not in the mood for humor, bantering, risqué, or anything else.

Nonetheless, when they got back to the villa, they made furious love, she as well as he.

CHAPTER SEVENTEEN

Afterwards, sitting on the edge of the bed, she asked, "Why was *I* so hot? *You*, I understand: all that testosterone. But me?"

"Danger. Relief."

"Maybe. Let me ask you something."

"Anything."

"When you call me names–"

"–they're *not* names, like that."

"–when you call me names–"

"–they're not demeaning. I have to explain that? You're the really smart one, and I–"

"I'm the educated one, that's all."

"That too, but you're bright on your own. So how come you don't understand times like that? It's part of your body, at that moment the most important part. It's you, you're it. That's all. And that's good."

"The way you said it?"

"Doesn't matter."

"I don't know."

"Well, it's never going to be cute, with me. No 'nest' and 'bird' talk." Then Sal sniggered. "Unless the eagle has landed."

Maureen hit him with a pillow. "You!" Then she said, "Something else. The truth is–"

"Oh, you were lying about something?"

"The truth is, I didn't actually mind you calling me that."

"Oh."

"But the other?"

"What other? What?"

"You know. All right, the midst of me, that's one thing. But 'whore'? You said I was your whore."

"No. I didn't."

"Yes. Talk *mama lucia*. Admit it."

"I said, wild whore."

"Big difference."

"Goddamn right! Are you crazy, or what?"

"Me?"

"Yes. Whore means prostitute, being paid for sex."

"And–?"

"*Wild* whore means doing what a whore does, meaning anything and everything. That's all. It was a compliment, damn it, maybe the highest. You were free. Hey, you're the grammar person. Everything was in the adverb."

Maureen fell off the bed.

CHAPTER EIGHTEEN

She had pasta from grocery shopping in Ocho Rios, and she prepared it the way he liked, with butter, then the grated cheese.

"Maybe they've got a spy in Ocho," she said, "telling them who's buying pasta recently."

"Ha," Sal said. "That's not the way it works. Buy all the pasta you want. But keep dyeing your hair."

After she served and they sat, she asked, "Sal, how did you get started with them?"

"Pure accident. Naw, there never is pure accident. Anyway, I was just out of the Marines. My oldest brother was in 'Nam ten years before and he stayed in the service, so I thought I'd try it, but I didn't go all that much for it, and I got out. I was in this club bar in Paterson–I was just in there–and Vinnie from high school recognizes me, he comes over, and we get re-acquainted."

"You started then?"

"About. It took a couple more times meeting there, joking around, playing darts, machines, and one night, outside in the parking lot, he asks me if I'm doing anything yet. I say no and he says, if I want, I could collect, the way he did, the mob was short-handed, and I just said maybe, and later I got introduced. The thing is, I look and smile the way I do, but I'm big enough, and He liked that, and I went in and worked myself up."

Maureen hesitated, then went ahead and asked. "Did you ever–"

"Off anybody?"

"Yes."

"Me, personally? No. Not then, especially–I was just collecting from the machines and for protection. You look the part, and maybe it goes perfectly all right." He paused, thinking back. "Anyway, I went all the way up to lieutenant, then, finally a junior *consigliore*. Until–"

"Never mind," Maureen said, "that's where I came in."

"Hey, it wasn't your fault that you were always around and we fell for one another finally, like that. It was nobody's fault. Accident. Co-incidence. Almost everything is an accident or co-incidence. Like my getting into the business, like I said." He paused, musing, "But that isn't the whole story."

"What do you mean?"

"I'll tell you. At the time, I could have gone in on something legit: Mitch Haley wondered if I'd like a job with him, in his father's S&L company. I was almost tempted, except for so much in-door routine. Later on, you know what? He finds out that, instead, I got into collecting, and he lords it over me, you know, holier-than-cow. It turns out, a few years on, his father is robbing the till and the S&L collapses! What did I mean, legit? There's nothing legit, not really, in the whole country. Everybody's stealing from everybody else. And that S&L hurt more people than we ever did. So, my mind's at ease in the big picture. In the local one, I was actually a good force, if you want to know."

"How?"

"As a matter of fact, some of the real goons will be glad I'm gone, because I was constantly stopping them from whacking somebody. You asked that before. I saved a lot of lives later, actually. The gorillas will be happy I'm out of their way."

"Not like this," she said.

"Oh, they don't care. *He* cares, but they don't pay attention to top-brass exchanges."

"Exchanges? Sal, we stole."

"Robbing the robber, it's not the same. I would never have done it, though, unless we just had to be together, you and me, get away together. If it wasn't for forbidden love, kiddo, I'd be in His Hq. and good graces yet. And don't say it's your fault again."

She got up and cleared the table. He helped clean up.

"You said you started on 'machines,' Sal. Slot machines?"

"No. It was pinballs. They were real money-makers for over a generation. We supplied them and took our 'commission.' But at least they gave a person some play. There was *no* fixed tilt, whatever you heard. Winning scores were set a little high, that's all."

"Why were you always mad at me for playing the slots, at Atlantic City?"

"Because it looks like action, but it's not."

"I never appreciated craps shooting. It's not lady-like."

"Neither is working a one-armed bandit. It's like jerking somebody off."

"Sal!"

"'Sal!' what? Not true? It's true. Anyway, don't trust *any* machine in gambling. That goes for the wheel, too. I guess," Sal was struck by his thought, "casinos, in Europe, are out also."

"Maybe we should have tried Puerto Rico. Did you ever consider it?"

"For a minute. But it's too close. And something else, kind of funny. The second part of the name, Maureen, is Rico."

"So?"

"You see, RICO is the anti-racketeering law that's been allowing the Feds to put away so many of the Family. The name put me off, mainly. So, we're going where I said, instead."

"Where are our passports actually getting made?"

"In Kingston."

"What about our pictures? Brunette and beard now."

"Believe it or not, I arranged for doctored photos when I handed ours over. If we don't like them, we'll just re-do them in Ocho. I know their contact man there, of course. Don't worry. And other documents, drivers licenses, like that. They're doing a slow careful job. We just have to sit tight. No, in our get-up now, we don't even have to do that these days. I got another place for us to go, another excursion, with a lot of people around, for sure, this time."

"Where?"

"A waterfall. You walk up, holding hands, all together. No lonely stretches with a knife man. We'll be all right."

"I hope so."

"What could go wrong in a big enough crowd?"

"*You* could go wrong."

"Stop."

"The old man said it, remember, when he said it's up to you. I think he meant, don't lose your cool and bring about a future you don't necessarily have coming."

"I think he meant…just keep my guard up. You know what I *really* think? I think he meant nothing. Just convenient words. *Con* is for *convenient.*"

"No. It's for confidence."

"Same difference. Anyhow, you want to just hang around here, or go out again?"

"Go."

"Good. I'll arrange it for tomorrow or the day after. The only thing is–"

"Don't tell me."

"What with the fire alarm and the river man–maybe it'll be something else–never two without three."

Maureen looked at him pityingly, a long look mixed with he didn't know what.

CHAPTER NINETEEN

At Dunn's Falls, there were a lot of people, all right. They held hands, making a linked human chain advancing up successive sprayed and slick terraces, one showery terrace after another, until the top. Strangers from different hotels and touring groups hooked arms or held hands for safety. On one side of Sal was Maureen, on the other side some foreigner. When they reached the third slippery level, the foreigner suddenly wrenched away from Sal, letting him go, flingingly, so that the torque spun Sal partly backwards and, on the slick rock floor, he let go of Maureen before pulling her down too, and he fell badly. More infuriated than hurt, he sought out the man on the top of the waterfall cliff.

"I was glad," Maureen said afterwards, "that you didn't throw him off the cliff."

"I just wanted to confront him, that's all."

"Slamming him into the luggage compartment of his bus sideways?"

"It turned out he was a German, and he waved me off with both arms, like he was dismissing me. I got mad at him."

"I'll say."

"For a minute there, on that waterfall, I thought maybe he was a disguised goon, the way he sort of flipped me. So maybe I was still thinking of that when I got back to him, on top."

"So you picked him up and threw him onto his baggage for two reasons?"

"Maybe. Actually I frisked him before I flung him."

"Great. You could be arrested one of these times."

"I got to watch that."

"You can get really violent, Sal."

"Under pressure. Just defensive."

"*Brutta,*" she said in Italian, looking at him with her skeptical ironic look, "maybe even *facia brutta.* Your new passport character beginning to come through?"

"Then I'll shave again. Hey, Maury, I'll be a sweet goddamn husband to you and father to your children in Switzerland. Give me a break."

"Let me look at your leg."

He pulled up his trouser leg. He had a bad scrape and a deep enough cut.

"You've been bleeding like that all this time! While we're talking! I'll drive. Get in the car. Give me the keys."

He handed them over, dutiful all of a sudden. "And you're soaking wet."

"So are you."

"Not *soaking*." She opened the passenger door and saw him in. "I don't think He'll ever get you," she said. "You're going to break all your parts or die of pneumonia first." She closed the door on him. Once behind the wheel, she said, "Another thing."

"What else?"

"Please don't call me Maury. Sometimes you do. It makes me sound like one of the boys."

"That you are not. You are definitely not. OK, I won't."

He sneezed. She was going to say something but did not. She drove back to the villa. They did not say anything. At the villa she shoved him into a hot shower and let him steam there a long time. They had a medical kit, and after his shower she salved the whole tube of polysporin in his scraped calf and cut shin. There wasn't a peep out of him. This was the high maternal side of her, but he did not mind. He was tired and hurting, and he did not mind, he did not feel put down or threatened. He felt comfortable, and thoroughly soothed. He sat on the bed.

"When we go for the passports and papers, day after tomorrow, in Ocho, you'll shop at the open market while I'm picking them up. That's all. Nothing'll go wrong. I guarantee."

"All I want is this: if you show up when I'm haggling over bananas, don't knock over the man's stall and throw him into it."

Sal could still laugh.

"Even if he's gypping you?"

"Gyp, gyp!" she exclaimed. "Our speech, our language is against everybody, what's the matter with us? Wop for you. Mick for me. Gyp for gypsy. All of a sudden sometimes I get mad."

"You do. I notice that."

"You don't give me any cause?"

"Wait a second a minute, I always have a reason. Suppose I show up and see he's making a pass at you?"

"Who?"

"The banana man, the cop on the beat, a passer-by, some pool-hall kid, anybody."

"I can take care of myself, that way. I always have."

"Suppose, at the vegetable stall, there's cannabis under the lettuce? And he points it out to you, with the end of his machete?"

"I can cope. You think that could happen?"

"You look like a mark."

"Thanks."

"No offense–I meant, just by being American. The way you're dressed, the way you walk. Funny thing, we're wops and micks and yids and pollocks and even chinks and spics, and you know what? We walk alike, we talk the same, they can spot us a mile off. We're Americans, and we don't know it enough sometimes."

"You're getting patriotic, or what? *Now*, when we've left the country?"

"No, no–I ain't sentimental. It was just a side thought. No, no, we're leaving it–and everybody."

"Sal, I'm an orphan. It doesn't matter so much. But you–?"

"I'll write cards and even telephone this relative or that. They'll hear from me. From out-of-the-way places. Say, Tangiers." That brought him back, though he felt heavy eyelids. "So somebody hits on you in Tangiers, or in Ocho here–"

"I said I can cope with any dealer. Oh. The other meaning, hit *on* me."

"Yes."

"I'll be all right. I'll be loyal."

"Good."

"Sal?"

"What?"

"Was He dealing drugs?"

"As a matter of fact, no. Not just that the Columbians got in control, but it was against His–"

"–principles? You've got to be kidding."

He patted his midriff. "No, I'm naturally fat." She did not get it or ignored it, intent on his main report. He went on: "All I'm

64

saying is, as far as I know, He never did deal, and the Jersey mobs before Him never did. Sure, originally they were bootleggers but, from what I learned, they never even drank, themselves. Wine, but never to get drunk on. When the drugs came in, He didn't want to deal, you know why? Because, after a while, the organization would be getting some cousins, some relatives, hooked. The old minorities–Italians, Jews, Irish too–never dealt drugs so much–for that reason mainly. Plus, He was already getting out of the rackets, mostly."

"What's going on then?"

"Gasoline is big now. Cigarettes. Small arms. Things like that yet. And protection, mainly He's always been into protection. And the piers still, in Newark and as far as Philly and Baltimore. But He's in construction, concrete, garbage disposal, laundry, legit businesses all over the place. Lots of straight money by now."

"Maybe He's got so much he won't miss the two million?"

Sal lay back on the bed, stretching out. "Up to a point," he said, "that's true. But He still has to go for it, get it back, because He's only chairman of the board, actually, not the owner. I'd say, deep down, personally, He's mad that I took the kitten more than the boodle." He closed his eyes and was asleep almost instantly on the bed covers.

She found a spare blanket on the shelf in the clothes closet and put it on him. "It's kit–and–caboodle," she told the dreaming man and kissed him lightly on the cheek.

CHAPTER TWENTY

Nothing dramatic happened at Ocho Rios. Sal limped slightly, but was free of pain and feeling good after a lazy night's sleep. He left Maureen at the busy central market and made his transaction. Their new American passports, with their new identities and the Jamaican entry included, looked first-rate and bonafide. "Craftsmen," Sal said, "you got to admit." And the pictures were fine, as he had predicted, and other papers also.

They went down the block to a bank for some more Jamaican money. Maureen waited outside in the tepid noon sun. Across the street were two American fast food places, McDonald's and, a little farther down, on the corner, a Godfather's Pizza. She recalled a Little Caesar's in Montego Bay. When Sal came out, they went to eat at a good seafood cafe.

There was a cruise ship in, and the seafood cafe was crowded for lunch. They were seated at a sidewalk table with a shipboard couple, who had little compact bikes loaned them by their ship; the miniature bikes stood like big toys near the table. Maybe for that reason the waiter was surly to the shipboard couple, or maybe it was because they were French and their French sounded highfalutin to him, or maybe it was their simple but stylish fashion. He was not too endearing to Sal and Maureen either. But with Maureen's hand squeezing his knee, Sal did not do or say anything. At one point the waiter said that something one of them ordered would be "too much," but none of the four could figure out what that was and whether he meant quantity or price. They all decided to be amused rather than angry. The meal itself was quite good. In the pleasant sunshine the two couples became fast temporary friends.

Toward the end of the meal, the French asked in their serviceable English where they might go scuba diving. Sal liked the idea himself. Maybe he could join them? Not today, they all thought, it would be too late, especially waiting out the two hours after lunch. They could reserve for tomorrow, the cruise ship still in port then. They all felt good about tomorrow morning. When they got their bills, there was an additional business card for scuba rental, put down by the sharp-eared but still unsmiling waiter. He had put his initials on it. They left him a full tip, after all, for the card (which they ought to give to the scuba man) and directions to the lagoon just outside of town where the scuba shop was, where they agreed to rendezvous right away. Sal drove over there, and the French couple came pedaling over on their low Singaporean bicycles, and they and Sal selected equipment and decided on ten o'clock the next morning. Everybody shook hands, and the French couple took off, pedaling back to Ocho and their ship.

"Aren't we getting social," Maureen said brightly.

"Why not?"

"And she's pretty, too."

"She's a pip. But you're pipper. Now, now, Maureen. They're in and out of this port in two days. C'mon."

"I guess that's right."

"You're not jealous, are you?"

"Would you be going with them tomorrow if she was a plain thing?"

"Of course. They're pleasant, and we all hit it off, one thing leading to another. Listen up: on hanky-panky, I trust you, you'll trust me. All right?"

"All right."

"You'll probably always be the best-looking woman. And I've got you, you're a beauty–*and* you've got a head on your shoulders. What else could I ask for?"

"A dowry."

"And I've got the dowry!" They were standing at the front of the car, and Sal folded over the hood, helpless.

Maureen laughed too and then didn't. "So we're getting back to normal?"

"Back? What do you mean, back? We've never been there yet. We're going *to* normal. I hope."

"What's 'hope' for?" It was a lovely marina, with a little beach off to the side, where Maureen decided she would sit the next morning. "You're still suspicious of anything, anybody? Not those French?"

"From the ship? No." He sounded withholding.

"What, *who*?"

"The waiter."

"The waiter? How can you think in a direction like that, even for a minute? *That* off-putting sneerer? And we came into that particular place just by accident."

"You're right. But if I was figuring odds, between a boat couple from Marseilles or an on-site person, I'd pick the waiter."

"And, then, the scuba man is going to fix your air tanks wrong?"

"In the realm of possibility."

Maureen shook her head more than once. "Here's a man running a business for who knows how many years and last week, say, He buys the operation, plus homicide services, plus the waiter–where He bought the restaurant, too?–plus a French couple, remember, who suggested the scuba diving–to get you to this lagoon tomorrow."

"Well, I'm going, aren't I? That means I don't believe any of it."

"Why even a flicker of a thought?"

"Because," Sal was fingering his half-beard speculatively, "I'm always on guard."

"Even if we're heading to normal?"

"We're not absolutely there yet. Although we're getting there. OK. And I've got this beard. Hey, let's look at the passports again, in the car."

Inside, looking at hers, Maureen said, "I don't look half bad as a red brunette."

"No."

"Angela Cahill. Angie. I'm an Angie."

"You're an angel. For the rest of your life."

"Oh? And you: what are you, who are you?"

He shoved her his passport again. "Francis J. Montefiore. It says here. The guy with the light beard."

"How do you do?"

They shook hands solemnly.

After an interval, Maureen asked, "What happens when we get married?"

"Oh, you wouldn't have to change it nowadays. Women are keeping their own names. I'll carry any kids, later, on my passport–little Montefiores. Simple."

"And when these passports expire?"

"We can't renew them. We're cut off from Washington. I'll find somebody in Europe by then, depend on it. Or the worst case, I'll fly back here for updating." He wondered aloud, "Ten years. Maybe there'll be no mob left–things are decelerating–and then we'll use the originals maybe. Don't throw them away."

"All right. We're all set then."

"Yep," he said, putting down his new passport on top of hers on the seat between them. "But if–" he sought the least likely scenario– "the French lady poisons my rum coke tomorrow noon, remember three things. Loose local cash is in this inside belt of mine. Heavy travel money is in my travelers checks, which you can redeem with a death certificate. And, don't interrupt, probably we already have our joint account–I'll have the number soon–under these new names in Suisse Banque in Lugano; relevant phone number and info also in my belt." He started up the car and then patted her thigh. "But that's just talk–in case I get pneumonia. OK?"

"OK."

Maureen registered what he'd said and then her mind fled it. Now that it wouldn't be long before they left Jamaica and everything seemed quite under control, she felt trembling inside her. She was nervous, not unnerved. There's a difference.

CHAPTER TWENTY-ONE

They waited until ten-thirty the next morning for the French couple to show up, but nothing happened.

"The little bikes aren't coming," Sal said.

"Maybe they got dates and ports-of-call mixed up," Maureen said. "Two whole days in Barbados, not Jamaica."

"No, the boat's still in, you can see it from here. They just finked out."

"Maybe they have a reason. It could be anything. They seemed nice. I have to admit."

"They finked out."

"Oh, my little boy," she said, patting him, "you lost your playmates. You want to go back home?"

"No. I'll do something here."

"Don't take the tanks, Sal."

"I won't. I'll just try that other thing, the periscope."

"You can't see out of it, you just breathe with it. It's called a snorkel."

"Yeah. Maybe I got enemy submarines on my mind. OK, I'll sit on the beach awhile with you and then go in the water."

Side by side with him on a big towel, she mused out loud, "Is this the way it'll be, snorkeling and sitting on the Riviera, then learning to ski in the Alps?"

"Not bad, is it?"

"No."

"I figure, we buy a house for half a million. Then, just leaving the rest at the bank, at six percent for the other million and a half, that's 90K a year. We can live on that. And if I figure out English or Italian football, that could be fifteen or twenty more grand."

"It's just that–"

"What?"

"It's not exactly a very productive life."

"Productive? Is that what they were dishing out in that night school at Passaic Community College last year?"

"Don't make fun of it."

"Productive! I should open a Savings and Loan of my own? Or make munitions? Or grow tobacco?" She did not say anything. "I see. You mean more like the other side of things, getting the cure for cancer so the cured can go on making the munitions and growing the tobacco. Is that it?"

"You're making fun."

"No. In the end, I'm not. By the way, I regularly coached basketball, to the YMCA kids, remember?"

"Yes."

"I'll probably coach somebody or do something in Lugano. There are leagues all over Ticino. Here's something else–"

"What?"

"I hereby pledge our first-born as a medical doctor. Boy or girl."

Maureen laughed a little. "And the second?"

"An engineer."

"Third?"

"Opera singer. No remarks."

"Fourth?"

"Big-time chef. Again, no remarks."

"Fifth?"

"All bets are off. We got us a basketball team."

Maureen laughed out loud, then bent sideways to kiss him. "You," she said.

"Listen," he said, "in all seriousness. About that doctoring: so it isn't just to patch up Mr. Colt or Signor Baretta or the head of Phillip Morris, but just plain people, too. So they can go on with their lives–their wage-slaving lives, with some nights off for basketball or whatever, and two weeks' vacation–for whatever available pleasure or joy they can get. Meanwhile, you and me will have that, that available extra. It's nothing to feel bad about." He kissed her on her cheek. "I feel good. On a day like this?" It was sparkling. "Really good. Even with a gimpy leg. I'm going in." He got up. "Hang out here and feel good. I'll be back in an hour."

When he got his mask and snorkel, he pointed to the coral rock wall around most of the enclosure of the lagoon of the beach, where he'd be swimming mostly, and then he put on his flippers and, under the scuba owner's gaze, swam a practice swim with the snorkel in the shallows and, five minutes later, after the owner approved, he lazed out further. He had gauze gloves on, she'd noticed, not to be cut by the coral and, sure enough, after awhile, he swam through the lagoon opening and around the coral wall to the right. Maureen watched from the beach, calmed but not calm.

He must have been out there, out of sight, a good half hour. She became restless. Then he was gone another five, maybe ten minutes. Despite herself, she felt nascent panic. Maybe she would go into the shop and say something. But she would not want to shame Sal. Maybe she could just walk a distance and then cross the base of coral wall and see over the other side.

But, then, what good would that do? There were other snorkelers all about and she had lost sight of his snorkel tube in particular. She noted that there were all kinds of yachts and boats about, with snorkelers and scubists around them in the far water and also near shore. She would have to wait. Another five minutes, say. Then she would saunter into the scuba shop and calmly, starting nonchalantly, begin to scream at the owner for help right away.

Afterwards, she would remember this time as her first swift premonition. Pretty soon a snorkel, *his* snorkel, she was sure, appeared from around the right-side coral wall, the swimmer–snorkel askew–swimming to shore with, seemingly, one arm doing most of the swimming, coming in slowly but erratically. Her heart started thumping.

She ran to the shop and cried, "My man," pointing to the lagoon. "Come!''

Her look and voice brought the owner out, and when they both got to the lagoon beach, Sal was trying to lift himself out of the water and onto the beach. His left arm bore a wound like a groove. There were strings of blood swirling in the water around and behind him.

Sal just lay on the beach, holding his arm. "Sonofabitch," he said but he was not swearing, only reporting, "shot me with a spear gun. I had to get in double quick–from a possible shark," he asked the owner, "right?"

"No, not this close," the boss said. "But from loss of blood, mahn. Good you swim in fast. Good you strong." He left and came back very soon with a roll of wide bandage. "Put it," he said to Maureen. "Tight. I call the ambulance." He went back to do it.

"Call the cops," Sal said, and passed out.

CHAPTER TWENTY-TWO

It was not so bad. The bleeding was well staunched before they got to the hospital, though he took several stitches after they cleared the wound.

"The wise guy who sewed me up," Sal said, back at the villa, "noticed the other bruises and said it all looked like domestic abuse to him." He sat in a beach chair and chuckled. "He gave me a shot too, for distemper or something."

It was one of those times: did he mean it, or was he kidding? Sal's half-ignorance was so cavernous Maureen got lost in it; only *he* found his way around in it. Still, he was almost everything else she wanted, including being her own age. If she could maybe just keep him here, here at the villa, safe and sound, avoiding all mishaps before they left the island, things would be all right. She could kick herself for urging them both out and around the way she had. Now he had final things to do in Montego and, anyway, could never be immobilized, though she'd try. "Tetanus," she said, but Sal was into his explanation.

"I'm coming around a corner and, just like that, whoof!–no, no, I never heard a thing–though I glimpsed somebody at the last second–something nicks me in the arm. Wow, the feeling. I half-saw the shooter. Either he never knew he hit me or he just zoomed out of there anyway, probably knowing he shot too close to a person, and he left. For a mini-minute I wanted to take off after him, and I think I even started to, but then I saw the red drifting around, out of *me*, and I thought of sharks, I didn't think of bleeding to death, but of sharks getting the scent, and I decided to come right in."

"Lucky you made it."

"If I could get my hands on that scuba guy."

"Or girl."

"Or girl. Oh: the French one?"

"I'm just talking," Maureen said. "Because how could it be?"

"No, it couldn't be. But if it *could*? If I was set up."

"How could it be? We already talked."

"Some masked man–his whole body in a mask, you could say–does me in, and who's to know what, where or when? Maybe I could've floated out further and the sharks *would* have got me. Then, no clue even. Perfect!"

"Sal."

"I'm Frank. I'm perfectly frank."

"You're the old Sal. Some scuba diver really aimed to assassinate you instead of just missing a damn butterfly fish?"

"Sure," Sal was laughing, though he dwelt on it. "Even without sharks finishing me off, the police would have figured I'd been wounded by the coral and fainted and bled to death. Or even if they figured I was speared, who are they going to arrest? Even if they found the spear. Doesn't salt water get rid of fingerprints?

What am I talking, there could be prints, but so what? Everybody's prints are on his own spear. *Whose* spear, from *what* customer who's gone home, from what diver who's gone to what boat that's sailed away? Perfect, absolutely perfect."

"Another accident. You're getting accident-prone, that's all."

"Sure. That's it. No question. After all. And Jeeves don't come into any of it."

Maureen was satisfied. He really knew it was a stupid accident. He knew, by now, that a total stranger had let go his hand at the waterfall, another sheer mishap. And he really knew that the raft poler was a small-time Jamaican hustler, trying something on the river, that was all. And the fire alarm just needed batteries. Everything was explainable. And Clive didn't come into it.

But what, Maureen thought, about her premonition, on the beach there? Oh that. Nerves, maternal feelings–and coincidence. She hugged herself now, on their own beach, their quiet peaceful beach, squeezing both elbows. Maybe she pinched herself, too.

CHAPTER TWENTY-THREE

He was well enough a few days later to go into Montego Bay for the Lugano bank account numbers, though Maureen drove. While she waited for him, outside a Cayman branch office, she felt like someone driving a getaway car.

It would not be long now, though they had decided to wait the extra week or so it would take for Sal's stitches to come out. He was basically all right. She was all right now, too. Nothing to be concerned about, all the things that occurred were just happenings. Something like them, although not maybe as frequently, would go on happening, in Switzerland, or anywhere. Life. She had the right perspective again. She was under control. So was he. And when Sal came out, he looked suave and smiling and erect, despite his wound and the pull of his stitches.

She stopped for ground meat and a little oregano and tomato sauce. Then she drove back to the house. Nobody rammed them. Nothing happened. She parked, they went in, she made Sal sit quiet in a chaise lounge on the beach, and made a lunch of spaghetti bolognese the way he liked it, not too sharp but grainy. Afterward, outside, the late sun shone down. Both of them were feeling fine.

The water in their little bay heaved blue, and the sea farther out glinted and sparked white where the breakers were. She held the sight to remember it.

CHAPTER TWENTY-FOUR

A day or so later she said, "I'm going to take a walk, along the side of the road, to St. Ann's–the other side of that Elderhostel."

"That's where the polo was. No more matches till next season," Sal said.

"Not for that."

"I didn't think so."

"I just want to stretch my legs."

"I'll come."

"Stay here. You need to rest."

"I don't. I'm coming. You make me suspicious."

They walked down their driveway, onto the road and then west past the neighboring compound and then another half mile or so to the village of St Ann. She eventually stopped outside of a church.

"I'm going in." Her low voice sounded sepulchral.

"This ain't no tomb," he said grinning, "lighten up. It's an Episcopal church, though."

"I know."

"But you're Catholic, kiddo."

"This'll have to do. Nobody in there is going to catechize me their way, *if* there's anybody. Sal, I just happened to notice it when we went to the polo match, and I want to go in and sit."

"I thought something like that," he said. "Sit? You're going to pray."

She did not answer.

"I'll wait out here," he said. "Take your time. You could've told me, Maureen, I would never put you down."

"You don't want to come in?"

"Go," he said.

Which she did.

She came back outside a half hour or so later, blinking her eyes for a moment against the sun. Sal was sitting on a low wall off to the side.

"You lost your religion?" she asked softly.

"Don't ask."

"It's just a question."

"Maureen, if the question behind this is about kids, no sweat. Baptize them (she would anyway, they always did, behind the backs of their renegade Catholic or their Jewish or their Protestant or Atheist husbands), send them to confirmation, bring them to communion. I won't give you any trouble. OK?"

"Aren't you Catholic anymore?"

"Sure. I'm just not religious."

"I don't get it." She stood next to him, the two of them in casual colloquy. He never lost his smile the entire time, although the corners of his mouth twitched slightly sometimes.

"I go to mass sometimes–say, at Christmas–for the sights and sounds."

"And? Go on."

"All right. You asked for it." If anything, he smiled more brightly. But he was not laughing. "If there is God–"he studied Maureen–"She's a gangster."

Taken aback, literally, Maureen said, "Sal! That's not funny, either way."

"Hey, you asked."

"How can you come out with something like that?"

"I think on my own sometimes."

"Explain it. For me."

"No big, deep deal. Hey: big-eyed, big-bellied starving babies in Africa or somewheres. It's pitiful. There isn't any God, Maureen, or, if there is, I don't want anything to do with Him, Her, It. Here's a thing: the Crusades–I once actually read a history assignment–talk about holy terror! And this century, the Holocaust, for Christ's sake. And kids blown up in downtown Oklahoma, with their teddy bears. And the World Trade Towers. I don't want to go on. I told you not to ask."

"I'm OK. What else?"

"You stopped believing in Santa Claus at about four?"

"Yes, about."

"Sure, people outgrow that. The thing is, they don't get past five, though." He looked at her steadily.

"Is that the rest of it?"

"Just add this. When some Sooner said that him and his wife were going to that Federal building that day but changed their minds at the last minute and went to the K-Mart instead, he said he had to thank the Good Lord for changing his mind and saving them. All right? Never mind what the Good Lord did to the others."

"People, people," Maureen said.

"Yep. *They* exist. But God? Like I said, I hope not. You believe, Maureen, way down deep?"

"I don't know. I'm afraid to go that far."

"Well, sure. You were brought up by strict nuns."

"It didn't take hold that much."

After a moment, Sal said, "Oh, well, you were looking for a father, an uncle."

"Yes," she said. "I guess so. Let's walk back."

On the way she said, "What about your immortal soul?"

"Listen," he said, "if you get up there, you'll put in a word for me."

She punched him on his arm.

"You're terrible," she said.

"No," he said. "I'm just not phony."

"No," she agreed, "you're not."

Me, she thought to herself, I've been taking the pill until last month. (And I haven't gone to confession for five years. I'm for women priests and I'm against the Pope. Coming in to a church off the street sometimes, sitting in the nice hush and quiet, praying even, isn't good enough. I don't qualify.)

To Sal she said, as they reached their driveway, "I won't really get up there either," pointing skyward.

"Does that scare you?"

She took a second or so to say, "Mostly, I don't think about it."

"Way to go," Sal said.

What passed her understanding was how to gauge his language, again. They went into their villa, their rented sanctuary just west of Ocho Rios. Another soft beneficence, with jasmine in the air, all day long.

CHAPTER TWENTY-FIVE

When the stitches were removed in Ocho Rios, Sal had Maureen in the room, too.

"Here's the woman who beats me up," he told the doctor.

The doctor had eyed her appreciatively. "I'd accept it, too," he answered.

"Damn right," Sal said. Then, "Ouch."

In the Ocho Steak House at noon, he pointed to another couple, in a booth not far away from them.

"See, she's sitting right next to him in the booth, holding on to him–see that?–batting her eyelashes up at him, the adoring mopsy. And he leans his head on hers sometimes, like a goddamn teenager. He's fifty-two, a clothier from New York, and she's his *zaftig* nineteen-year-old idolizing muppet with the outsize knockers, which is his big interest."

"What's hers?"

Sal looked all around. "*This* place. Or Puerto Villarta. Or Bermuda. Or, when he visits his sweatshops–all the world is rackets!–Bangkok or Hong Kong or Singapore, she goes, too, hanging around in a swank place. He's loaded. Take a look at the ring."

"She's carrying a big sparkler, all right."

"Not her, *him*: the diamond on *his* pinky. And the Rolex watch. And the gold ropes around his neck."

"Sal?"

"What?"

"Are you prejudiced?

"Where did that come from?"

"You meant *Jewish* clothier."

"Is he? I'll go over and ask him." Sal started getting up.

"Sit down."

Their margaritas and salsa chips came.

"Listen, Maureen. You know damn well I had Jewish friends and acquaintances. For crying out loud. And don't I know how much the ethnics get along now–Jews, Italians, Irish, Polish, everybody. There's even inbreeding all over the place."

"Inter-breeding."

"What I said. You know Kevin Greenberg, in Englewood. And who was that nice guy in class with you at Passaic Community–Emilio McCarthy? And, just before we left, I came across a Gustaf Marionzetti. All right? All of us getting really together now."

"Including you and me."

"Right."

"The thing is, Sal, sometimes, like just before, you think in stereotypes."

"Wait," Sal said earnestly. The steaks had arrived. "Thanks," he said to the dark waiter. When the waiter left, he said, "See? No stereo stops me from saying thanks nicely."

"Big deal."

"No, don't brush me off. No matter what, every time I meet a person–white, black, brown, yellow, he could be aquamarine for all I care–one on one, me and him, all stereos are out. I hope it's the same for him. I say to myself–no, I don't even say anything, I just act on it–this is a person in front of me, unless or until he proves otherwise–this is a particular person, a human being, and that's first and foremost. In fact, that's all. Now, is *that* prejudice?"

"No."

"All right. I'm sorry that I crack some jokes and I say this or that sometimes. But I try to be fair in my own mind. I try to be: personal. Listen–"

"I'm listening." She was, smiling, seriously too. She would never clamp his arm or bat her eyelashes up at him.

"Did I act wrong with the old black man in the woods?"

"You were a big-shot American once or twice there."

"Oh yeah, I could be that with anybody. That's the me I'm trying to get over."

"You thought of him as a, you know, witch-doctor."

"Ah, Maureen. Didn't we always pass remarks against Auntie Viola in *Sicilian* Paterson? I can be a smart alec against everybody, even my own. And the old man in the woods? I actually liked him."

At the end of the meal she said, "Am I a stereo if I take one of these Jamaican liqueurs they have?"

"Oh, on top of the margaritas and the wine we had? Go ahead. I won't, I'm driving back. No, actually, you're no Irish drinker, Maureen. I've noticed. I hope Angie Cahill won't be."

"Don't worry."

"Good."

When the drink came and she sipped it appreciatively, she said, "These conversations we've had. I've gotten to know you better. Like on a honeymoon."

"My guess is, couples don't have these conversations on their honeymoon."

"Maybe not."

"It's more like–like we had a whole lifetime of talking together, in Ocho Rios and all around where we've been here, this month. That's nice."

"Sal, I want to tell you something, one thing."

"What is it?"

"You've made me feel...un-lonely."

His heart swelled, then completely melted. But there was the table between them. And, considering the clothier and his mopsy, his self-respect. He did not lean to kiss her or anything. All he said was, "Yes, me too."

He paid the bill and left a tip more like twenty-five percent, and they left.

Walking toward the car in silence, he kept thinking toward something, then came upon it.

"Something the old man said about me, I think against me," he reminded Maureen.

"Oh. Was *he* a racist?"

"No, as matter of fact. The waiter we had here in Ocho with the French couple, he was a racist. But the old man asked if I was Italian Italian or American Italian. He was against me as an American. You see, not that they don't have other reasons, but I found out that the Reynolds Aluminum plant here just pulled out in a dispute they had, leaving 'em flat. A lot of lingering resentment."

"He was against you as an American?"

"Sure. Hey, didn't I look like the American New Yorker–" he thumbed back to the restaurant they were in– "with my big money and whole attitude in there? You yourself said big shot. Italian, Jewish, hillbilly big shots: We have to get over that."

"Don't worry about it."

"I'm not worried. Just talking." He put his arm round her shoulder, then withdrew it but not before he stroked her hair once. "Get your hair dyed all the way tomorrow. It's still off a shade from the picture."

She nodded. "Where will you be going?"

"No where. I'll loll around the place, like I've been doing. Perfectly safe. Like you want."

"Oh? Good!"

"We're on our way, Angie."

"Thank God."

Sal did not say anything. He opened the car, and they got in and drove back.

CHAPTER TWENTY-SIX

While Maureen was in the beauty parlor chair next morning, Yolanda, her cheerful hairdresser, kept fingering her own right ear. She shook her head a few intermittent times, backing off from the tinting job to do so. She came back to Maureen.

"Water in my ear," Yolanda said.

"Oh, my husband had it, a while back. It can hurt a lot."

"Oh yes! Just before it's over it's the worst. Like now. If I could only shake it out."

Maureen stiffened in her chair. "How do you know that the worst time is what you said, 'just before it's over'? How do you know that?"

"Two weeks," Yolanda said. "Lots of people on the island know that. Water in the ear can't last no more than two weeks. But it hurts like the devil just three days before the end."

"My God!" Maureen said. "The old man gave him a placebo, a placebo powder."

"Who? I dunno what that–"

"Never mind! Just finish the tint," Maureen said, "*please.* I've got to get back home for something, all of a sudden. *Hurry,* please!"

*   *   *

At the villa Sal had put on his blue floral trunks. A steady
strong breeze blew from the East, churning up rills of waves and
rattling a group of short palms on the left and one taller sole palm
on the right. He wanted to sunbathe. He was outside, on the coarse
gravelly sand, preparing a toweled place to sit or lie down,
thinking he could just as well be nude in this secluded place, he
didn't need to wear anything, except that he actually did not like
sand in his loins, and he went on stretching the towel flat—when he
glimpsed something. He stood quickly up, tensed.

He glimpsed it again: out in the cove, from the left, around
the shoulder of low coral wall, there—there again—something, a
form, had bounced into split-second view and back off again, a
form. Sal whirled and regained the house.

Inside the house Sal searched for his little hip pack, where he
kept his wallet, travelers checks and gun—*where* did he put it last?—
and he also concentrated hard on what he had just seen outside—
rummaging, rummaging around the bed, around his nightstand for
the pack—had seen a form bouncing in and out of view at the corner
of the cove, a human form—strange—no pack in the bedroom, he had
had it on in the kitchen, at breakfast: look there—the form was a
man hunched over: on the sea? how?—not anywhere in view in the
kitchen, the pack nowhere at or around the table or anywhere on
the floor—on a raft, a little *raft*, hunched over on a raft, with
something, a weapon—oh, he had taken both his pack and bathrobe
off near the sliding doors of the living room, where he put on his
trunks, without picking back up—weapon, a long rifle across his lap

or across the gunnels of the little raft, at the ready–the .38 from the pack that he now zipped open after finding it half way under the drapes of the living room doors, grasping it now, looking outside–there, to the left, seeing nothing now–still seeing nothing, but dashing out.

He cocked the gun, running back out, onto the beach, making sure that the safety was off, heading for the one palm on the right where he could steady himself and get the first good shot off, and then–he saw–just then–the raft floating back, curiously or cunningly, into view, and the hit man, his head bent forward on his chest, looked up, the whole raft now definitely into the cove–floating, bouncing, in the secluded bay–the man seeing Sal bracing himself for a two-handed aim, the man raising his own weapon and firing first but missing–and Sal also missing, the raft and the man in it bobbing, bobbing–and the sun aglitter on narrow folds of tiny waves with slim whitecaps–and they shot it out, very unprofessionally, awkwardly even, but continuously.

CHAPTER TWENTY-SEVEN

When Maureen took the turn into the villa driveway, she had to stop abruptly for two patrol cars, one athwart the driveway. The police had been called by the Elderhostel personnel, who heard the shooting, even saw the first part of it, their somnolent guard on the compound's raft having drifted all the way over to their neighbor's, then getting into a crazy, prolonged fire fight, disappearing completely and noisily around the coral wall there. Then silence, and they called.

The police took Maureen inside the house. They would not at first let her see Sal, crumpled on the beach under the palm tree. Then, for recognition, they did. She held his head in her lap. "You," she said, and she kept whispering "You," in his ear, "you, you." His head lay on her lap, the rest of him limp on the coarse sand. His face, even bearded, looked somewhat surprised.

She laid him down gently back on the sand and stood up. Did you have any thoughts? she asked him silently. No, I know you, you didn't have any thoughts. You didn't *think* anything, did you, not in any kind of action you ever were in. And you didn't know anything, my handsome boy, you didn't know that the man happening to hold a rifle on the little rocking rubber raft was another accident, you jittery beautiful man, thinking if you had any thought at all that there wasn't any time for thinking but only acting, but maybe thinking–once, Sal–of me, maybe that I was safely out of it, away from the hit. Were you glad of that, Sal, something like that? You were one split-second glad, Sal, you were glad, you were.

CHAPTER TWENTY-EIGHT

When the Chief Inspector for the north counties of Jamaica, out of Ocho Rios, showed up, he had his own look around and talked with junior officers and detectives, and then he came into the living room, where she sat.

"There is no crime here," he said, "actually. Two dead men in what one might call a float-by shooting. Big mistake. No crime."

Maureen said, "The butler did it."

"Excuse me?"

She shook her head. "Nothing."

"I am quite sorry," the Chief Inspector said. "Only one thing. The Elderhostel guard had an authorized weapon. Your husband had his pistol from where?"

Her mind was back. "You know from where. From here. It's that kind of make, isn't it?"

"Why—may I ask—did he acquire a gun here?"

She looked up at him. He wore a neat, crisp blouse, creased unwaveringly all along each sleeve, with platform epaulets on top, and had a thin mustache and friendly but almost unblinking eyes. "Are you joking?" she asked him. "There was armed robbery at a private house not far from here, a month or so ago. Some Canadian tourist girls were raped on this side of your island. There are armed guards posted in hotels and educational resorts. Please!–do you have the expression we have in the States?–give my man a break.''

"Yes, of course. Where did he get it?''

"How should I know? He went places when I got my hair done, like that. He also got killed while I had my hair done."

"I am truly sorry. Very regrettable. The two men misunderstood each other."

"I'll say."

"We shall proceed to take them now. Is that all right? And you, of course, are free."

"I want a plane out of here. Right away." It would not be long, of course, before this news story got out.

"I understand. You will stay for the funeral and then depart."

"I want him cremated, right away. Then I simply must leave this place."

Beautiful woman, truly beautiful, tear-streaked, utterly bereft. How sad and truly touching to the Inspector. "I shall contact airport authorities not to slow you in any way when you present your passport." His men had probably searched the house for drugs, just to be sure.

"Thank you," she said.

"Not at all. Are there any calls we may help you make?"

"No."

"Is there *anything* I can do, Mrs.–"

"Cahill," she said.

"Yes. I wonder–I wonder if I could just confirm your passport? And take his, please? If it's not too much trouble now? Just a formality." He glanced all about the room. "There is actually nothing to investigate further." His English was impeccable, though there was still a very slight lilt in it. "We'll be going shortly."

She gave him her new passport, which he read quickly and then returned. And she found and gave him Francis J. Montefiore's passport. If only because the beards matched. "Will you be taking the–gun?" she asked.

"Oh yes."

"I see."

"Ah. You are afraid to stay here alone, perhaps. There are no rapes or robberies quite hereabouts. You won't need–"

"No? How about the dead guard's brother? Or an Uncle. Or somebody....What do you know about that guard?" she seemed to run on, "how long was he employed over there, recently or what? Who is he, who are his relatives?"

"We know about him very well. Do not be troubled on that score."

"Good to hear. Sorry about him, then." She waited.

"I will not say it was a fortunate death, because–how can that be, for anyone? But he was, himself, elderly–that, in particular, was why he was napping on his raft–and, we have learned, he was suffering a terminal though not painful malady. It turns out that he was insured by the American compound, the Elderhostel. Rather exceptional for Jamaican families. His relatives will be quite surprised and not–not despondent. I don't mean to be heartless, for he will be mourned very properly, but that insurance, you see–"

"I see."

The Chief Inspector straightened his shoulders. "Nevertheless, I shall have a policeman on the driveway. For peace of mind, and for–" he calculated the coroner's report, the death certificate registry, and cremation–"three days. You'll fly then?"

That would have to do. She nodded.

After they left, except for the officer posted on the driveway, she went to the bedroom and she sat on the bed. She held her elbows, squeezing in on herself hard. "Jesus, Mary, Joseph," she said out loud, softly. Then, with both hands, she caressed the bedspread on either side of where she sat, keening voicelessly.

Sal, she thought: Sal, you brought it on yourself. And you've left me. She squeezed herself again. "What's the good of two million, with the entire boodle on my hands? Without you, Kitten?"

And three more whole days here. She began to blubber, her nerves shot. She held her elbows again, trying to contain herself, her midriff. "Sal," she asked the pillow on his side of the headboard, "can I make three days? And the rest of my life? Almost all alone?"

END

www.ingramcontent.com/pod-product-compliance
Lightning Source LLC
Chambersburg PA
CBHW072034170626
46811CB00008B/3082